Christopher's Story:

A Dog's Walk Through John 3:16

By Terri Blazell-Wayson

Acknowledgements

Thank you to my husband for sharing his wife with her computer and giving me the time and space needed to write this book.

Thank you to the many people who were a part of our story. Your love and faith brought me through. And to Celebrate Recovery for giving me a voice and allowing me to explore creative ways of sharing my story.

Thank you to Jesus who redeemed me.

A special thank you to Jessica Bateman and Ruby for allowing me to use Ruby's photo on the cover. The only picture I have of Christopher is an old, faded Polaroid.

Christopher's Story:

A Dog's Walk Through John 3:16

If there were a hinge in the Bible it would bend right at John 3:16. Everything that comes before this verse is the tragic history of mankind; how we turned away from God and made His perfect world into something imperfect and every person born into it broken.

And then we turn the page:

For God so loved the world
that he gave his one and only Son,
that whoever believes in him
shall not perish but have eternal life.

History bends right here and mankind goes from lost to found, hopelessness to hope, unloved to unconditional love.

About Christopher

But the wisdom from above is first pure, then peaceable, gentle, reasonable, full of mercy and good fruits, unwavering, without hypocrisy.[1]

This is the nature of God but doesn't it also perfectly describe the soul of a dog? It certainly describes Christopher.

I think God pours a bit of Himself into every dog.

Christopher was a gentle, floppy-eared mutt who came into our lives in the 1970s when I was a struggling teenager. He was a wise, loyal dog; our "peace maker."

This is Christopher's story "in his own words.'

---

[1] James 3:17

My story begins long before I was born.
But, then, all stories do. – Christopher

1971

"For God So Loved…"

Imagine you are a good Christian family. The husband works, the mother stays home with your five kids and you love the Lord. You read from the Bible after dinner and pray with your children at bedtime. You faithfully attend church every time the doors are open; Sunday morning worship, Sunday School, Sunday night, midweek prayer meeting, Vacation Bible School, Choir Practice and more. It's what a good Christian family does.

You're not rich but you manage to make ends meet and you are happy with what you have.

Then one day, the rug gets yanked out from underneath you. The husband gets laid off, inflation and unemployment are soaring and the price of gas is at an unthinkable high of thirty-nine cents a gallon. You hang in there for as long as possible but no one is hiring, nothing opens up and before you know it, you're behind on your rent and you can't pay the electric bill. You have absolutely no where to go. Like Job, you're trusting in the Lord but you can't help but wonder "Why is this happening, Lord?" and "What did I do wrong?"

Finally the husband is offered a job in a town far away that you've barely heard of at a much lower salary than before but at least it's a paycheck. You pack up your belongings; cram the kids into the twelve-year old station wagon with thread bare tires and head out hoping nothing breaks down and you'll have enough money along the way to keep gas in the tank.

When you roll into town, you are shocked. The town with the pretty name, Garden Glen, is a dump. There are bars, laundry mats and run down homes nestled among sparse dehydrated trees and layers of grime and graffiti.

And worse, you can't afford to rent anything decent. The cheapest place you can find is a row of small, dilapidated studio apartments with broken sidewalks, broken beer bottles and broken people. It's the type of place that sometimes gets rented by the hour. You eye the run down tenants who shuffle in and out of one apartment or the next. You think about your children. You think that in your whole life, you would never, ever bring your children to a place like this.

You have to decide between living in your car and living here. You reluctantly choose here.

The apartments are closets; one single dingy room taken up almost entirely by a shabby double bed, a tiny kitchen and a tinier bathroom. You have to rent two of them side-by-side just to make room for your whole family and it is still cheaper than anything else in town. Plus it's the only one where the landlord is willing to wait on the rent until your first pay check.

You think a little about Joseph and Mary and you're grateful your wife isn't nine months pregnant. Still, it's 105 degrees as you gloomily unpack your things. The husband goes off to work and the mother realizes that as much as she wants to avoid contact with the world outside those walls, it is too stifling hot to cram six people, five of them hyperactive and stir-crazy in a single room and still keep your sanity. She prays a lot under her breath.

So she plops a folding metal chair outside against narrow a planter full of dirt, rocks, and one dust-choked cactus. She sits with her arms crossed against her ample chest; the guardian of her brood, staring out across the cracked asphalt and gravel parking lot that is your new front yard.

The kids do what kids do. They run around and make up games and climb the lone tree that gratefully casts a sliver of shade right in front of your place. Surprisingly, out of a nearby apartment as equally pathetic as your own, maybe more so because it doesn't even have a tree, steps a little girl. She is small with limp blond hair, dirty feet and knitting needle thin. She has the appearance of a Dickensonian street urchin. Somehow the words scraggly and scrawny come to mind but there is also a toughness about her like a weed desperately surviving in the crack of a sidewalk.

She eyes your kids, both curious and suspicious, before walking barefoot across the molten asphalt towards you. You guess her to be about eight or nine but later find out she is almost twelve.

Of course, your kids gravitate to her and while your instinct is to herd them inside, you know that it would only delay the inevitable. You find out quickly that she has the mouth of a sailor and the manners of a billy goat. You wonder if you can afford enough soap for all the new words you're going to be washing out of your kid's mouths. You also discover a little later that she is fatherless and her mother is an alcoholic.

That little girl is My Girl.

Now, let's freeze this moment right here and step backwards one year in time.

The little girl is living in a different dilapidated apartment in a different heap of a town. She gets up in the morning, dresses, eats a cold cereal breakfast, makes a white bread and jam sandwich lunch and takes herself off to school. Her mother is either passed out in the bed or on the sofa. On good days, her mother is alone. Some days, she isn't. Sometimes it's someone who's been there before and sometimes someone new but they are all alike; gaunt, stubble and the unmistakable smell of dried urine and alcohol.

After school the little girl comes home. Typically, her mother is gone. She is off cleaning houses and afterward at the bar. The little girl does her homework, goes out to play with the neighbor kids till dark then watches TV and makes herself a canned soup dinner before going to bed alone.

The next morning, she awakes to find her mother isn't there. It happens sometimes. She doesn't need her mother very much. She follows her routine and when she returns home from school, it's to an empty, untouched apartment. She doesn't mind. Being alone is better than having to deal with her mother's drunken episodes; the screaming, the crying, the vomit. And it's especially better than having any of her mother's male friends there. They do things.

But this time days go by. She starts to feel a little lonely; a little worried. On the third day after school, there is a knock on the door and a policeman is standing there. Someone reported that a little girl was home by herself. This little girl is terrified. Strange men are scary. Policemen are scary. And no matter how terrible a mother she is, she's all you've got. You still love her and you would cling to her with your dying breath rather than be dragged away into the unknown. So she does the only thing she knows to do; she lies.

She tells the policeman that her mother has been leaving early in the morning for work and working till very late at night. The policeman tells her that he will come back later that night and if her mother isn't there, she will have to come with him. The door closes and she is left standing there in the growing dark.

The little girl looks around the dirty, lonely apartment. There is no one to turn to or talk to. She is all alone. Then she does something that she had never been taught to do. She didn't even know where the idea came from but it was there like a light in the room. She got down on her knees and she prayed a simple prayer.

"If there is a God, would you please bring my mommy home?"

She went through her routine as if nothing had happened. She played outside under the streetlight with the neighbor kids, saying nothing about the policeman. She did her homework, ate her dinner and watched TV. She kept her eye on the ticking clock.

Then the door opened and her mother was there acting as though she had only been gone an hour. She mentioned casually that the car had broken down but the little girl knew that any other mother would have done anything, *anything* to get back to her child and not leave them alone for days.

She wrapped her arms around her mother and had barely finished telling her about the policeman and the clever lie she had told him, when there was a knock on the door. It was the same policeman and he looked quite relieved that he wouldn't be hauling away an abandoned child this night. She peered out into the darkness as her mother confirmed her lie but the little girl was only half listening. A sentence was running through her head over and over again.

"There is a God and He heard my prayer."

Now, let's fast forward to that one year later. To that family with their five kids. The little girl made friends quickly. Kids just do that. The mother watched for a while, listening, observing the type of girl that was raised in place like this. Then she picked that little girl up – it was like lifting up air- and sat her on her large, fleshy lap covered by a flowery cotton muumuu. She dabbed her sweaty forehead with a handkerchief and did what she had done to every child that had ever visited her home in the past. She took hold of the little girl's hand, looked into her eyes and said, "You are loved."

"From the very beginning, before He even created this world, God loved us and had already chosen us to be His very own. [2]

"The first two people He made, Adam and Eve, were supposed to take care of the perfect world that He created just for them. But they disobeyed Him instead and sin came into the world. It is the root of every bad thing that has ever happened. When they had children, their sin was passed from person to person to person. We can't wash it away or just make it go away."

This little girl knew about sin. She knew about the lie she had told the policeman and many, many more; the ones she couldn't tell anyone about.

---

[2] Ephesians 1:4

"It not only ruined this world but it made us slaves to that sin and our master was the devil. But God never stopped loving us and He wanted us back. But He'd have to pay for us." The mother wrapped her arms around her and spoke softly to her.

"Jesus, God's own Son came to earth and lived with us. He saw firsthand what sin had done to us. He healed the sick. He fed the hungry. He gave sight to the blind. The lame could walk. And He loved everyone He met. He didn't care if they were poor or old or sick. They were all His children."

"But the most important reason He came was to save us. He would pay the price for our sins; His life for ours. One day, angry men took Him and nailed Him to a cross. The whole world grew dark as all the sins ever committed came to rest on Him. He was the sacrifice that would take our sins away."

"He gave up His life to save ours. It was His way of saying "I would rather die than live without you." They buried Him in a cave and rolled a huge rock in front of it. For three days His friends and family wept. They had given up hope but on the third day, He rose from the dead! He was alive! It was the proof that He was who He said He was."

All the while, a sentence was running through the little girl's head, "This is the God who heard my prayer."

"Now, all we have to do ask Him to forgive our sins. And He will, just like that. He will never leave us and we will live forever in Heaven with Him where we'll be safe and happy and will never cry or be hurt again."

She said a simple prayer and that little seed that had been planted in her a year before, "There is a God and He heard my prayer," blossomed into a new life. On the outside it didn't change much. Her mother disappeared on and off again. There were other strangers. They moved from one shabby apartment to another. But that family got her rooted into a nearby church where they looked after her like she was their own.

As for that family, is it no surprise that the father found a better paying job soon after that? They moved away and she never saw or heard from them again. She wonders if they ever realized that all of their hardships that Summer so long ago were so they could be missionaries to the most unlikely of little girls.

And here is where I come into the story.

1973

"The World…"

My earliest memory was riding in a car. I was just a puppy. I don't remember anything about the people in the car or my life before that day. I just remember the car slowing down, the door opening and I was thrown out. I howled as I hit the pavement and rolled over several times before coming to a stop on the side of the road.

I was scared and I hurt all over. I sat there on the hot sidewalk and licked at the scrapes on my legs. I didn't know where I was or what I was supposed to do. I kept telling myself over and over again:

"Be strong and courageous. Do not be afraid or terrified because of them,
for the LORD your God goes with you; he will never leave you nor forsake you."[3]

Those words are in the Master Creator's book. When Adam and Eve sinned, the words disappeared from their hearts and had to be written down. But they are still buried deep in the hearts of all His creatures.

I decided that I would be strong and courageous.

---

[3] Deuteronomy 31:6

I didn't know where I was so I got up and started walking. I hadn't gone far when I saw My Girl. She was sitting on her front porch, her elbows on her knees and her face in her hands looking so forlorn. When she saw me, she ran right over and scooped me up. She smelled like bubble gum and peanut butter, loneliness and someone with a desperate need to be loved.

She also smelled of something else buried deep inside of her. Everlasting Life. My Girl belonged to the Master Creator! I wriggled with joy.

The Master Creator's book says *"I found the one my heart loves. I held him and would not let him go*[4]*"* and *"God sets the lonely in families.*[5]*"*

I knew immediately that this is where the Master Creator meant for me to be.

She carried me into her house. I hadn't been in a house before so I didn't know what to expect. It was small and cluttered and smelled of so many things; dust, cat poop, talcum powder, bacon grease, shoes, and many things I couldn't identify.

---

[4] Song of Solomon 3:4

[5] Psalm 68:6

There was stuff everywhere –all over the tables, shoes and clothes thrown on the floor, pillows and blankets on the sofa, boxes full of stuff stacked up against the walls. Even an ironing board in the middle of the room piled high with clothes. Every horizontal space was piled with things and covered with a layer of dust and cigarette smoke.

My Girl took me into the kitchen. It had dishes stacked in the sink, more on the counters and all over the table. There were boxes and cans of all sorts of food, cups and saucers, pots and pans. I noticed a lot of things were cracked and chipped. I wanted to examine every bit of it but I was hungry. My Girl must have sensed it because she rummaged around and mixed together some dry cat food and chopped up boloney.

"I'm sorry," she said. "We don't have any dog food."

It was the best meal I had ever eaten in my entire life.

My Girl played with me for the rest of the day. She took me outside and showed me where I could pee. Apparently only cats are allowed to pee in the house – in a stupid little box. As it was getting dark, she made me another delicious meal of dry cat food and boloney.

While I was eating, the front door opened with a bang. I jumped and My Girl stiffened. Standing in the doorway was the weariest person I would ever meet. I instinctively knew that she was the Alpha of this pack. She smelled of alcohol and cigarettes, and pain; the heavy, throbbing kind buried deep in the soul.

She also smelled of perishing. Perishing people don't know the Master Creator's love that forgives sins and gives eternal life.

My Girl was very tense. She had her arms crossed in front of her and anxiety seeped out of her pores and filled the air. I sat at her feet looking up at both of them.

"Mama…" My Girl said in a small, timid voice.

Then the Alpha Mama saw me and shouted, "Oh, Christopher! What is that?"

And that's how I got my name.

"He Gave His One and Only Son..."

I loved my pack. We were family. They were good to me. Sometimes they weren't so good to each other, though. Alpha Mama would come home smelling like alcohol. And My Girl would be so angry. My Girl would shout at her for being drunk. Alpha Mama would shout back that she wasn't. My girl would bring her food to eat. Sometimes Alpha Mama threw up. Or she just lay on the couch, barely breathing. My Girl would cry and scream at her. Sometimes Alpha Mama sobbed and nothing could make her stop.

When My Girl went to bed, she would wrap her arms around me and tell me things.

"Why did my dad leave me? What did I do wrong? Does God know what it's like to be me?"

If only she knew...

If only she knew that the Master Creator knows exactly what it's like to be her.

"The virgin will conceive and give birth to a son, and they will call him Immanuel" which means "God with us...and he gave him the name Jesus"[6]

My Jesus.

What would My Jesus know about a teenage girl's life?

He knows what it's like to not fit in.

Can you imagine what His brothers and sisters thought of Him? Kids stay out of trouble by getting someone else into trouble. And they always hate the one who doesn't get blamed for anything. Can you imagine My Jesus – perfect in every way - never disobeyed his parents - always good and helpful? Mommy's favorite. Can't you just hear it? "Why can't you be more like your brother Jesus?"

They probably looked for ways to frame Him and blame Him for stuff He didn't do. They probably left Him out of a lot of things – didn't want Mr. goody-two-shoes interfering with their plans or taking all the fun out of it. Perhaps He was the one sitting all alone in the corner reading while the other kids played outside without Him.

---

[6] Matthew 1:23,25

He also knows what it's like to not belong.

I'm sure Joseph was a good father but he was also human. I think there might have been times when he looked at My Jesus and thought to himself, "That's not my son." Joseph was a carpenter and usually the first born son was trained in the father's trade but in all of My Jesus' parables and stories, he never talks about carpentry. Doesn't that seem strange? Perhaps Joseph waited to teach his trade to the son who looked like him with daddy's eyes or daddy's nose while My Jesus stood on the "outside looking in."

My Jesus knows what it's like to not have a father at all.

We don't know when Joseph died but after My Jesus turned twelve, there is no mention of His earthly father. When he performed His first miracle, turning water into wine[7], only His mother was there and on that tragic day when My Jesus died on the cross, He gave his mother into the care of his friend, John, because Joseph was no longer there to take care of her.[8] My Jesus was missing two fathers – the earthly one chosen to care for Him as a child and His Heavenly One so far away.

Oh, yes, My Girl. He knows.

---

[7] John 2:1-11

[8] John 19:26-27

In the morning, she would get ready for school. My Girl and Alpha Mama would pick up right where they left off the night before. Alpha Mama was angry that My Girl had left her on the couch and didn't help her into her nightgown and into bed. My Girl was disrespectful and yelled back that it wasn't her job. My Girl would call her a drunk and yell things at her that she shouldn't yell at her Mama no matter what.

Alpha Mama would yell at My Girl that her pants hung too low and she shouldn't bare her midriff like that. Or that she was staying too late after school. That she didn't like the way she talked back to her or that she needed to help more around the house. My Girl complained that her clothes were all hand-me-downs and yell at Alpha Mama that she should get rid of all her junk so that she could clean up the house. They were both so angry.

Broken people break others. Hurting people hurt others. And these two were broken and hurting.

My Girl would slam the door as she left for school. I would sit on the couch next to Alpha Mama. It was her turn to cry.

Alpha Mama would tell me about her hurts and fears. A failed marriage and raising a teenager all alone. She loved My Girl but didn't like how disrespectful she was. She worried about the bills and making ends meet.

She didn't like getting drunk but it made her feel less lonely. It made her forget. She felt so lost and thought no one knew what she was going through.

But My Jesus knows.

My Jesus knows what it's like to be in a bad marriage. Surprised? He knows what it's like to have a relationship start out with someone seeing all the good in you and then time goes by and something shifts and all they can see is what's wrong with you.

My Jesus loved Judas as deeply as He loved anyone but Judas saw what he perceived as faults and weaknesses so he walked out on the relationship. He betrayed it. He destroyed it. Sadly, he didn't stick around to see how My Jesus would have restored it.[9]

---

[9] Luke 22:1-6 & Matthew 26:47-50

My Jesus knows what it's like to have an addiction. More surprised? He spent forty days in the desert with the sun beating down on Him; no food and no help. As the days passed, the hunger kicked in; a gnawing, clawing agony that started in His belly and crawled up His throat.

As the days turned into weeks, his hands began to tremble and the ache in His head went from a buzzing to a pounding to an endless throbbing. Insomnia and sweating tormented His nights.

After a month, He was a wasted, skeletal figure with a racing heart thumping so hard against His ribs He thought they'd break. He lay rolled into a fetal position, shaking and rocking, feeling like He was going to die. And at the end, wishing He would.

Throughout it all, that little voice begging Him to have just one taste; one little taste. The Devil laughing and holding out a loaf of bread, daring Him, begging Him to take just one bite.[10]

My Jesus knows all about addiction.

---

[10] Luke 4:1-13

My Jesus knows what it's like to have children go astray, to hate you and blame you for their lives and their mistakes.

"Hear me, you heavens! Listen, earth! For the Lord has spoken: I reared children and brought them up, but they rebelled against me."[11]

Yes, My Jesus knows all about our struggles here on earth.

[11] Isaiah 1:2

Things weren't always bad. Sometimes Alpha Mama didn't come home smelling like alcohol. She was a wonderful cook and we had the best meals. They always shared with me. They would watch TV together and I would sit between them. Both of them rested their hands on me. We were connected.

On Sundays, families from church would pick My Girl up and take her to church. She always came home very thoughtful. She would try to clean up the house. She would pick up the clothes, wash the dishes and put them away. Sometimes, she would dump the broken things into the trash.

But when Alpha Mama came home, she wouldn't be happy. She would yell at My Girl for throwing away her treasures then she would dig through the trash and pull them back out.

I think Alpha Mama saw herself in those broken things. If broken things could be thrown away so easily, what about broken people?

"That Whoever ..."

One night Alpha Mama brought a stranger home.
Her arm was crooked in his and they were singing and
leaning on each other. Alpha Mama's familiar odors were
mingled with his - alcohol, tobacco, sweat and motor oil.

But the strongest stench was lust; a thick, musky
haze that rose up from both of them. I felt the fur rise up
along my back fifteen hairs at a time. I was on alert.

My Girl grabbed me by the collar and dragged me
into her room. She closed her bedroom door and padlocked
it shut then reached under her bed and pulled out a stick.
She placed it under her pillow and went to bed with all of
her clothes on. She lay there staring at the ceiling for a
long time.

I could hear slurred voices and laughter in the next
room.

My Girl stared at the ceiling. Then she wrapped her
arms around me and cried into my fur as her fear turned
into a deep, piercing pain.

My Jesus knows that pain. My Jesus knows what it's like to be abused. When they arrested Him, they stripped off His clothes, they beat Him in the face, and ripped out His beard by the handfuls. They taunted him, spit at Him, kicked Him and beat Him with whips. They nailed Him to a cross and laughed at Him. And finally, they thrust a spear into His side.

Yes, My Jesus knows our pain. He felt our pain. He took that pain as His own; took it to the grave and left it there.

My Girl tried to stay awake but finally her eyes shut and she fell asleep. I stayed awake for her listening to the strange sounds on the other side of the wall. Very early in the morning I heard the front door open and close.

The Stench had left the house.

"Believes ..."

Sometimes, the people from church would visit Alpha Mama. They would invite her to church but she mostly said no. She would go at Christmas or Easter when My Girl had a part in a play or sang in the choir. My Girl would practice in her room and I was her audience.

Alpha Mama listened from the living room. She was so proud of My Girl that the air around her smelled like she had rolled in clover but My Girl didn't realize it.

"I don't belong there," Alpha Mama told me once when we were sitting on the couch together and My Girl was at school. "They're good people and I'm not."

Oh, Alpha Mama, the Master Creator loves you just as you are. When Jesus walked the earth, He loved the thief, the prostitute, the poor, and the damaged. The hungry, the blind, the broken-hearted and the run-away. He loved the addicted, the grieving, the angry and the untouchable.

And He even loved the repeat offender. Those so caught up in their pain and their past that all they can do is repeat their vicious cycles over and over again. Those weighed down with their shame and guilt, unable to lift their head or feel any sense of hope that the cycle can be broken. The Master Creator is the only One who can take it away. No one else can do that.

There is a neighbor dog that lives down the street. She got a flea bite on her leg and kept chewing on it. The more she chewed, the more irritated and raw it became. And the more irritated it got, the more she chewed on it. It was a vicious cycle. I thought she might chew off her leg. But you know what? Her Master never stopped loving her. And her Master slathered her leg with ointment and tenderly wrapped it in bandages so it could heal.

The Master Creator is like that. He never stops loving His children and He provides healing, not condemnation.

The church people were kind to Alpha Mama. They made her feel welcome even if she didn't dress or act the same as they did. One Sunday when she went to church to hear My Girl sing, she heard John 3:16 for the first time. Or maybe it was the hundredth time. I've noticed that dogs can hear everything but even though people have ears, they don't always hear with them. No matter how many times Alpha Mama might have heard it before, this time she really heard it because the scent of it was still on her when she came home.

For God so loved the world that He gave
his one and only Son,
that whoever believes in him
shall not perish but have eternal life.

My Jesus said those words.

Imagine Him standing in front of that crowd. He's looking out at them and what does He see? He sees the blind and sick that He had healed but who never came back to say thank you. He sees the people He fed who went away filled but quickly forgot His message. He sees the crowd who a week later would cry out "Crucify Him!" Those who would rip the beard from His face. Those who would laugh while he was being beaten. Those who would scoff when they laid His bloody back down on a plank of raw wood and hammer spikes into his hands and feet.

He stood in front of that crowd and He said to them -

"For God so loved the world that He gave His one and only Son."

For God so loved the world – how much? THIS MUCH! And Jesus stretches out His arms.

"That he gave his one and only Son that whoever believes in him shall not perish…"

A person doesn't have to die or go to hell, to perish. Alpha Mama knows what it feels like to perish –that weight of guilt on her chest that is always pushing down; the burning and hurting and being eaten up from within. The ache that gnaws and won't go away. It's to die a little every day. She goes to sleep perishing, she wakes up in the middle of the night perishing and she makes it through her days perishing.

And not just Alpha Mama – but everyone - until they find Jesus.

And there stands Jesus with His arms open wide, "Whoever believes in me shall 'stop' perishing!"

The perishing stops right now. He will come into your heart and start the healing. He will quench the fire and stop the bleeding. He will end the addiction. He will heal the broken. His blood washes away the hurts, hang ups and habits that claw and burn and cause you to perish every moment of every day.

"Whosoever believes in Him shall not perish but have everlasting life."

Perishing doesn't start when you die – it has been in you all along. And the everlasting life doesn't start when you die either. It starts the very moment you bow your head and cry out, "Jesus, have mercy on me, a sinner."[12]

If He can forgive the sins of those who put Him on the cross, there is nothing anyone has done that is so bad that He can't forgive you. Jesus starts walking beside you on this journey that is everlasting life. It starts right now. The transformation begins now.

That's how much He loves you.

---

[12] Luke 18:13

1975

"In Him…"

The people from church kept inviting Alpha Mama to come back but it took a long time. One day, when My Girl was at church, I lay next to Alpha Mama on the couch while she ran her fingers through my ears. I knew that John 3:16 was on her mind because the fragrance was there.

"Do you really think God could love me? After all the things I've done?"

I snuggled up next to her. I loved her unconditionally and I'm just a dog.

Yes, Alpha Mama. He loves you.

Listen to John 3:16 with your soul. Listen to it with your heart. Listen to it one more time in its deepest meaning.

"Our Master Creator
so deeply loves this world He created
with His very own hands that
when He imagined each person and creature
who would one day be on it,
He fell all the more in love with each one and said,
"Yes, you. I want you to be on my planet
to enjoy all the amazing things
that I created just for you.
And I will create a path
and plan for each one of you
that will bring you the greatest purpose
and deepest hope.
So He breathed His life-breath
into each person and creature that He made.
There was Life!
And when that Life rejected His love
and the world turned upside down,
the only thing that would save it was to allow
His Son to pay the price
for all the sins of the whole world.
The Master Creator gave up
His One and Only Son.
And My Jesus came – and lived – and healed – and loved.
Then My Jesus stretched out
His healing, loving arms
and let them be nailed to a cross.
He died for the whole world!

But He took death with Him and buried it.
He rose from the grave and left death there.
And it will be buried forever.
Then there was no more perishing.
The perishing ended and the healing began.
'Look!' He said when He stepped out of that grave.
'Death was just a shadow and now it is gone!'
So believe!
Say it, 'I am loved! Loved by the One and Only.
The Shepherd and the Lamb.
The Heavenly Father and His Son.
And there is nothing that can separate us from that love.
The perishing has ended!
Eternal life and eternal love have begun."

And THAT'S John 3:16! I don't think humans use enough words for that verse.

One day Alpha Mama decided to go to church when it wasn't Christmas and it wasn't Easter.

I don't know all that happened there but when Alpha Mama came home from church that day, she glowed. She had stopped perishing. She smelled of eternal life. Now they both did!

I wish I could say that things were perfect after that but life isn't like that. Humans aren't like that.

Along the side of our house, from the front porch to the back door, is a trampled dirt path worn through the grass; hard-packed over the years from the footsteps of My Girl and Alpha Mama. And me. I've run around that path many times. Nothing can grow there.

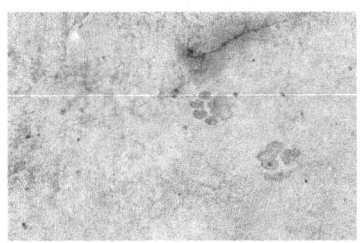

People are like that. They have paths worn into them from hurtful people, harsh words and their own repeated mistakes. They are scars and no matter how thick the grass grows, those scars remain buried just underneath.

That's the way it was for My Girl and Alpha Mama. They trampled on each other's scars and lashed out at the pain. But they were slowly healing. And My Jesus comes along beside them and walks those paths with them.[13] He makes new paths.

In time, Alpha Mama didn't smell of alcohol or cigarettes as much. The magazines with movie star faces disappeared and were replaced with a Bible that she read nearly every day. She started throwing away all those broken things that she had treasured so fiercely; the ones that My Girl had tried to throw away so many times before. She had found a new worth. She didn't need to hold on to broken things any more.

We spent more time sitting on the couch together. More time eating meals together. More time watching TV together. For the first time, there was more peace than pain.

---

[13] Psalm 23: 2

My Girl and Alpha Mama went to church together. There were moments of real peace among the turbulence.

But they were still mother and teenaged daughter, and mothers and daughters butt heads. My Girl was growing up. She didn't want Alpha Mama telling her what to do. Alpha Mama still saw her as her baby girl. Every day was a tug of war and there was a lot of hurt they had to let go of along the way. They didn't know it then but it would take the rest of their lives.

It was all a part of their redemption story. A story that began at the beginning of time and will go on forever. But they made it, one step at a time. And before I knew it, My Girl was heading to college.

1978

"Shall Not Perish…"

The crows on our street drive me crazy. They pluck a walnut from the neighbor's tree, fly up high over the street and drop it. It hits the asphalt with a whack and breaks apart. Then the crows fly down and pick out the nut meat. All day long they do this. Drop. Whack. Swoop. Nom-nom.

Today is the day I'm going to catch one of those crows.

I waited at the edge of my yard.

Drop. Whack. Swoop. Nom-nom.

Drop. Whack. Swoop.

I rushed out into the street. I was going to catch a crow.

I was so focused on those shiny black feathers and beady eyes I didn't see the car until I heard the screech of its brakes. I didn't even have time to look up.

I felt the heavy thud as I was crushed into the pavement and the tires rolled over me.

It only hurt for a moment. I closed my eyes and felt the warmth of deep, enveloping love surrounding me and the bright light of my pathway upwards. My Master Creator was bringing me home.

My Girl was going off to college and Alpha Mama had a new family in the loving people at the church. My journey here was done.

I will miss them and I know they will miss me. Oh, how My Girl and Alpha Mama will weep for me. But my Master Creator knows best and when He says my service here is completed, it is completed.

I can't wait for that pat on my head or hear those words, "Good boy."

2013

"But Have Eternal Life."

As you can imagine, a lot happened over the years. My Girl grew up and Alpha Mama grew old. The journey of Faith involves a lot of falling down and a lot of getting up. When you have Jesus, you have faith. When you have faith, you have hope. And when you have hope, you always get up. They fell down a lot but they always got up. And that's what matters.

In April of 2013, Alpha Mama stepped into the outstretched arms of My Jesus. Before she left, she was surrounded by My Girl and other loved ones. They sang hymns and held her frail, wrinkled hand. They prayed over her and blessed her. And then she closed her eyes and was gone.

I raced over to her the moment she arrived in Heaven but I wasn't the first one there. My Jesus got there first. He always does. He wrapped his arms around her and held her. I slipped in between their legs and stood there leaning against them.

My Jesus held Alpha Mama and slowly her soul filled up with His love until there was no room for the ugliness of her past. Each moment on earth was lifted away, replaced with beauty and acceptance. The scarred, worn paths of earth were gone. Everything she had endured, that had twisted and imprisoned her– abuse, hunger, fighting, screaming. War[14], alcoholism, regret, abandonment, rape. Grief, weariness, bitterness, rage, anger; even a miscarried child. This would be the last time she would ever feel that pain. She was a new creation; the old has gone.[15]

With each memory, she wept. Big, glistening tears welled up and slid down her cheeks while her body heaved with sobs as she relived her life. Tears rolled down her face into My Jesus' hands. He held them gently as one who has wept. Finally, she stopped crying. There was no more sorrow. No more pain.

I don't know how long they stood like that. In eternity, it is hard to gauge time but I suspect He held her for as many years as she had lived. When it was over, Alpha Mama glowed. She was no longer old or crippled. She was beautiful. It reminded me of another verse in the Master Creator's book.

---

[14] Alpha Mama was born in Germany and was nine years old when WWII started. She had shrapnel scars down her back from when she dived under a truck during an air raid and the truck was blown up. She had many such stories from that time in her life. The trauma never left her.

[15] II Corinthians 5:17 Therefore, if anyone is in Christ, the new creation has come. The old has gone, the new is here!

He will give a crown of beauty for ashes, a joyous blessing instead of mourning, festive praise instead of despair.[16]

Finally, Alpha Mama noticed me. She bent down and wrapped her arms around my neck, buried her face in my fur and held me. She breathed deeply and it was the breath of someone who was finally at rest.

Master Jesus touched her shoulder and said, "Someone is waiting for you."

As Alpha Mama stood up, a smiling, young man walked towards her. I wagged my tail. I couldn't wait for her to meet him. We have spent a lot of time together since I arrived.

"Mama!" He grabbed her and held her tightly to him.

Alpha Mama stared at him, her eyes wide as comprehension slowly flooded in.

"My son?"

---

[16] Isaiah 61:3a NLT

Alpha Mama touched his cheek and looked at him in awe.

"My son?" she asked again. "How can it be? You were never born?"

"Oh, I most certainly was," he said. "A life is a life no matter how brief."

"My son!" She cried again but these were tears of joy. He touched the tears and stared at them for a long time. He had been in Heaven his whole life so he had never seen a tear.

They held onto each other for as long as they had been apart. When finally she could let him go, knowing they would never be apart again, Alpha Mama looked up and there was a whole multitude of people waiting to see her.

Her own mother, healed and transformed in the same way My Jesus had restored Alpha Mama. Now they could love each other unconditionally as they never could on earth. Family members. Friends. People she had hurt. People who had hurt her. Her father whom she had never known. And on and on; even people she had never met who had been a part of her story long before she was born.

They are still hugging and laughing and loving on each other.

And that is where my story ends. But as you can see, it never ends, does it?

"There is a God and He hears my prayers."

Terri Blazell-Wayson

John 3:16 According to Christopher

"Our Master Creator
so deeply loves this world He created
with His very own hands that
when He imagined each person and creature
who would one day be on it,
He fell all the more in love with each one and said,
"Yes, you. I want you to be on my planet
to enjoy all the amazing things
that I created just for you.
And I will create a path
and plan for each one of you
that will bring you the greatest purpose
and deepest hope.
So He breathed His life-breath
into each person and creature that He made.
There was Life!
And when that Life rejected His love
and the world turned upside down,
the only thing that would save it was to allow
His Son to pay the price
for all the sins of the whole world.
The Master Creator gave up
His One and Only Son.

And My Jesus came – and lived – and healed – and loved.
Then My Jesus stretched out
His healing, loving arms
and let them be nailed to a cross.
He died for the whole world!
But He took death with Him and buried it.
He rose from the grave and left death there.
And it will be buried forever.
Then there was no more perishing.
The perishing ended and the healing began.
'Look!' He said when He stepped out of that grave.
'Death was just a shadow and now it is gone!'
So believe!
Say it, 'I am loved! Loved by the One and Only.
The Shepherd and the Lamb.
The Heavenly Father and His Son.
And there is nothing that can separate us from that love.
The perishing has ended!
Eternal life and eternal love have begun."

In Heaven, Children
By Terri Blazell-Wayson

In heaven, children climb upon God's lap.
They run their fingers through His beard
And weave daisy chains for His hair.
They look into His eyes and smile.
He tickles them and they giggle like little chirping birds.
Stop and listen when birds sing;
It is our children laughing.

In heaven, they reach up and take the hands of angels.
They go for long walks
and sail banana leaf boats on Heaven's lake.
They splash the water
with their pudgy hands until it splatters
over the sides, down to earth.
Hold out your hands and feel the rain;
It is our children playing.

In heaven, children run barefoot through the warm grass.
They flop down in it with their chins in their hands
While bees buzz about their heads.
Bees never sting in heaven, they only kiss.
The children hold hands in a big circle
with God in the middle.
They sing ring-around-the-rosie.
When they all fall down it sounds like thunder.
Smile when it thunders.
It is only God and our children playing.

In heaven, angels tuck our children
into the clouds for their naps.
They rock them gently to sleep with the breezes.
When they awaken, it is still day,
For in heaven it is never night.
Close your eyes and feel the wind on your face.
It is rocking our children to sleep.

In heaven, no one ever hurts a child.
Never makes them cry.
In heaven, they are safe
And warm and loved.
It is all they know, for God makes it so.
They call it Home
And play hide-and-seek around God's throne.
Someday we will go there.
Our children will come running out
with arms open wide,
Shouting, "ollie ollie oxen, Free!"

~~~

Thank you for reading Christopher's Story; A Dog's Walk Through John 3:16. This was a tough story to write; reliving those moments that I would rather have left in the past. But I hope that in telling them, that others will find hope in a God who loves them and a Savior who died for them.

If you enjoyed this book, you might like my other book, Lisa's Testimony; A Dog's Walk Through the 23rd Psalm.

* The name Garden Glen is fictional so as not to hurt the feelings of the many good people who live there today.